No Fits, Nilson!

Zachariah OHora

Dial Books for Young Readers
an imprint of Penguin Group (USA) Inc.

For Lydia, who deserves more credit.
And Oskar, the sweetest gorilla.

DIAL BOOKS FOR YOUNG READERS

A division of Penguin Young Readers Group • Published by The Penguin Group • Penguin Group (USA) Inc., 375 Hudson Street, New York, NY 10014, U.S.A. • Penguin Group (Canada), 90 Eglinton Avenue East, Suite 700, Toronto, Ontario, Canada M4P 2Y3 (a division of Pearson Penguin Canada Inc.) • Penguin Books Ltd, 80 Strand, London WC2R 0RL, England • Penguin Ireland, 25 St. Stephen's Green, Dublin 2, Ireland (a division of Penguin Books Ltd) • Penguin Group (Australia), 707 Collins Street, Melbourne, Victoria 3008, Australia (a division of Pearson Australia Group Pty Ltd) • Penguin Books India Pvt Ltd, 11 Community Centre, Panchsheel Park, New Delhi - 110 017, India • Penguin Group (NZ), 67 Apollo Drive, Rosedale, Auckland 0632, New Zealand (a division of Pearson New Zealand Ltd) • Penguin Books (South Africa), Rosebank Office Park, 181 Jan Smuts Avenue, Parktown North, South Africa, 2193 • B7 Jiaming Center, 27 East Third Ring Road North, Chaoyang District, Beijing 100020, China • Penguin Books Ltd, Registered Offices: 80 Strand, London WC2R 0RL, England

Text and pictures copyright © 2013 by Zachariah OHora

Designed by Lily Malcom • Text set in Imperfect • Manufactured in China on acid-free paper • 10 9 8 7 6 5 4 3 2 1

    Library of Congress Cataloging-in-Publication Data
OHora, Zachariah.
  No fits, Nilson! / by Zachariah OHora.
    p. cm.
  Summary: Amelia must continually remind her gorilla friend, Nilson,
not to have fits, especially when they are running errands with her
mother, but sometimes Amelia stomps and growls, too.
  ISBN 978-0-8037-3852-2 (hardcover)
  [1. Behavior—Fiction. 2. Gorilla—Fiction.] I. Title.
  PZ7.O41405No 2013
  [E]—dc23   2012021514

The artwork was created using acrylic paint on Stonehenge printmaking paper.

Nilson and Amelia
do everything
together.

Except for baths,
because Nilson is afraid of water.

It's all fun and games, but
sometimes all it takes is a
tiny bump . . .

BUMP

and Nilson throws the biggest,
most house shaking-est fit ever!!

So big, they **BOTH** get a time-out.

Sometimes Amelia tries to help Nilson
when he starts to get upset.

"No fits, Nilson!" she'll say.

"We're having banana
pancakes for breakfast!"

Banana pancakes make Nilson forget all about his fit.

After breakfast, it's time to help Amelia's mom.
But Nilson wants to stay home.

"No fits, Nilson!" Amelia says. "This
is an ADVENTURE, not errands!"

Nilson is perfectly behaved at the grocery store.

But he is ready to burst while they're waiting in line at the Post Office.

GAARRRGGHH!

"No fits, Nilson," whispers Amelia as she hands him her favorite froggy coin purse.

He's patient waiting for the train and even holds the door.

But on the train someone else has a banana. Uh-oh! Nilson really wants a banana, too!

"No fits, Nilson!" hushes Amelia's mom. "If you both sit quietly, we'll get banana ice cream on the way home."

Amelia covers Nilson's mouth and stares him down with a gorilla eye lock, repeating the words banana ice cream over and over.

At last! Their stop! At the ice-cream truck
Nilson places his order.
"Here you go, last scoop of banana, folks!"
sings Albert the ice-cream man.

Amelia can't believe it.

She stomps.
She growls. She roars.
**"I WANT A BANANA
ICE CREAM!"**

That's when Nilson hands
her his ice cream.

"No fits, Amelia!"
he says. "I'll get
chocolate instead."

"Thank you,"
Amelia peeps.

They both share cones, and guess what?
They have a new favorite flavor!

Choco-Banana-Twist!

That night Amelia gives Nilson an extra hug.
"I love you, No Fits Nilson!" she whispers.

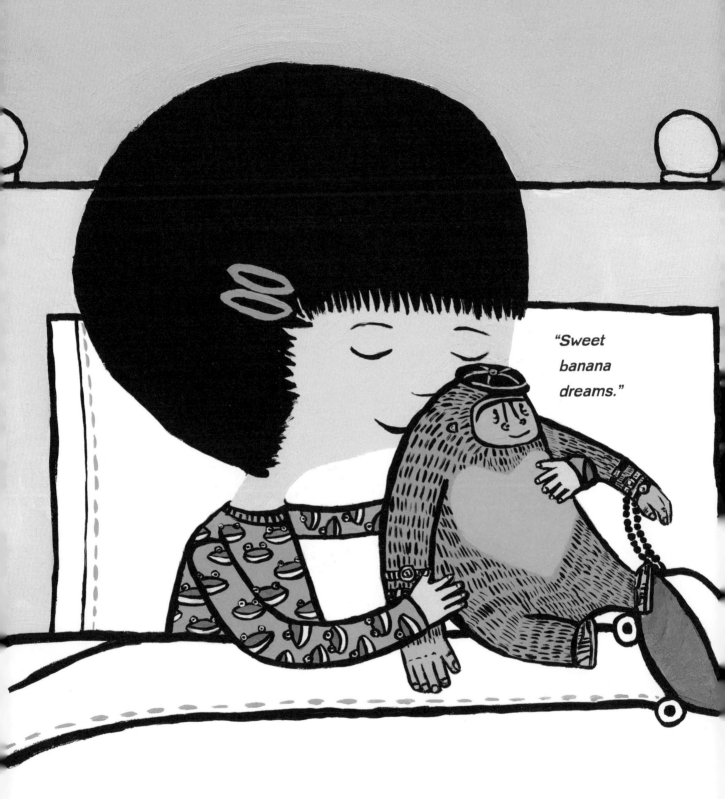

"Sweet banana dreams."